Adventure At The Popham Colony

This is the story of the adventure, struggles and tragedies of the Plymouth Company's first settlement attempt in North Virginia.

Enduring fire, death, bitter weather and abandonment, the Popham Colony set the stage for the successful settlement of Plymouth Plantation by the Pilgrims.

ISBN # 0-8059-9627-3
Printed in the United States of America

First Printing

For information or to order additional books, please write:
RoseDog Books
701 Smithfield St.
Pittsburgh, PA 15222
U.S.A.
1-800-834-1803
Or visit our web site and
on-line bookstore at www.rosedogbookstore.com

Adventure at the Popham Colony

by Alex Popham King

RoseDog❖Books

PITTSBURGH, PENNSYLVANIA 15222

CONTENTS

Introduction

In the year 1607, the Jamestown Colony was settled. However, Jamestown had a twin colony and as sometimes happens with twins, one lives and one dies. This is the story of Jamestown's twin, the twin that died.

The Popham Colony was settled in Northern Virginia in what is now known as Popham Beach in the State of Maine, at the mouth of the Kennebec River, then called the Sagadahoc River.

Its principal backer was Sir John Popham, the wealthiest man in England at the time. Sir John organized the Plymouth Company, along with family members, investors and adventurers. His nephew George Popham was the president of The Popham Colony.

The winter of 1607-8 proved to be one of the harshest winters ever recorded in America or in Europe. Due to this misfortune and other overwhelming challenges, The Popham Colony only persisted for a little over one year.

The Popham Colony was not, however, a total failure. Much knowledge was gained from this venture. Knowledge that proved invaluable to those settlers that later pursued settlement attempts.

The first ship built by Englishmen on the shores of the New World was built at The Popham Colony. She is named *The Virginia*. She was a thirty-ton pinnace, fifty feet in length and was a fine seaworthy vessel.

Little is known of her history, except that she made at least two Atlantic crossings. Her first Atlantic voyage took some of The Popham Colony colonists back to

England and her second resupplied the Jamestown Colony. Little more is known of her history. Her replica is currently being constructed.

Both The Popham Colony and The Virginia of Sagadahoc were commemorated by the issuance of an U.S. Postal Service commemorative stamp in 1957 on the occasion of the 350th anniversary of these events.

The exact location of The Popham Colony was uncertain for many years. In 1888 a map of the colony, drawn in 1607 by Mr. John Hunt, was found in the Spanish Archives in Simancas, Spain. Ongoing archeological excavations under the directorship of Dr. Jeffrey Brain of the Peabody Essex Museum, Salem, Massachusetts, have uncovered the exact location of the colony. Current work is underway and much new information is being discovered. The National Geographic Society, Maine State Museum and State of Maine Historic Preservation Commission have supported the excavation.

Thirteen years after The Popham Colony, in 1620 the Pilgrims would establish their colony within the boundaries of the Plymouth Company's land patent.

For more information, please visit our web sites at www.pophamcolony.org and www.mainesfirstship.org.

Chapter 1

AN INTERESTING OFFER

It had been raining all morning. This is rather common weather for the West Country of England.

Around midday my younger cousin knocks loudly on the door. He exclaims, "Benjamin! Benjamin! your Uncle George Popham sent me to get you. He has something he needs to discuss with you."

"Uncle George has something to discuss with me?" I think to myself. Being only ten years old, I am not accustomed to adults discussing things with me.

I quickly slip into my slicker and run to my uncle's home. Wild thoughts are running through my head.

Uncle George is an important man. He has held many high governmental positions. What could he possibly have to discuss with me? While he has always treated me well, I thought he hardly knew I existed. I met Uncle George only two years ago when my parents died and I came here to live with my aunt.

When I arrive at Uncle George's home, he is looking out his front window. A slight smile is on his face. He opens the door and welcomes me inside. His home is warm and cozy. Getting inside out of the drizzle feels great. He welcomes me, "Take off your slicker and come sit here by the fire. We have some important business to discuss."

When I am settled into the large leather covered chair by the fire, Uncle George begins to speak. "Benjamin, you are a sturdy young man with a good head on your shoulders. I have also noticed your keen interest in ships.

King James has granted your Uncle Sir John Popham and Sir Ferdinando Gorges permission to settle colonies on the coast of the New World in a place called Virginia. They have organized *The Plymouth Company* to build the colony and have raised money and obtained the needed ships for the venture.

Uncle George Welcomes Me Inside

Virginia stretches hundreds of miles from the French territory in Canada at the north end, southward to the Spanish Territory.

One group of men will settle a southern colony to be named Jamestown.

Raleigh Gilbert, Sir Walter Raleigh's nephew, and I will take 125 men to settle a northern colony named The Popham Colony after your Uncle Sir John Popham. We will build a fort to protect our colony. The fort will be called Fort Saint George, after the patron saint of England. Sir John has been a main supporter of the project. He has contributed much influence and money to this venture.

I will be captaining the sailing ship named *Gift of God* and Raleigh Gilbert will captain the ship named *Mary and John*. This is a very large and important adventure. It will require much preparation and there will be a lot of hard work.

I will need a dependable assistant to aid me in many ways. After considering all the young men in the town of Plymouth, I've decided I would like you to be my cabin boy. Are you interested?"

I couldn't speak. This was like a dream come true. I had wondered what I would do with my life and I do love the tall ships. I said," Yes, yes, I would be happy to serve you in this adventure."

Uncle George Popham replies, "Thank you Benjamin. I am quite pleased you will be working with us."

We will be leaving by the end of May, which only gives us a few weeks to make the ships ready for the voyage. We have a lot of work to do.

Between now and then, I will need you at the Plymouth docks every day watching the preparation.

You will need to learn the ship from bow to stern. I will depend on you to know where all the various supplies are stowed.

Mr. Digby will be there tomorrow tending to preparations. He is from London and is a fine ship's carpenter. Mr. Digby will be in charge of making repairs while we are under way and will supervise the construction of a new ship after we land in Virginia. I will tell him to expect you tomorrow morning."

Chapter 2

GETTING PREPARED

Arriving at the dock very early the next morning, I find the sky clear and the sea calm.

The *Gift of God* is a grand ship and looks very large from the dock. Her tall masts look as if they could touch the sky. On the top of the tallest mast I see the crow's nest from where a sailor acts as lookout. "What a beauty she is!"

On board men are busy at work. "Ahoy," I holler, "I'm looking for Mr. Digby. Can one of you gentlemen tell me where he is?"

"I am he, one of the men yells back. You must be Master Benjamin, Captain Popham's cabin boy".

"That I am, Sir," I reply.

"Well come on board and get acquainted with some of your shipmates."

Mr. Digby is a stocky man, with huge muscular arms and a happy face. "I am going to like him," I say to myself, as I climb up the gangplank to the main deck of the ship.

Mr. Digby is the ship's carpenter. He will be in charge of keeping the ship in good condition during the voyage and will repair any damage that might occur while we are at sea. His helpers are loading lumber and materials that Mr. Digby may need. He is busy checking the ship over and making certain she is in the best possible repair before we leave.

Iron fittings and sail material for the ship that will be built at the new colony are being carefully stowed in the hold.

The dock is a flurry of activity. Men are filling the hold with provisions for the journey and for the new colony.

Large heavy cannons are being lowered into the hold. Other munitions include long guns of several kinds, lead for musket and pistol balls, cannon balls and gunpowder.

Food is mostly dried, salted and pickled. Axes, shovels and other construction tools are loaded.

Some provisions are packed in curious green glass bottles that are actually made square to fit neatly into wooden cases. Others are in fine ceramic containers. Pickled fish and meat are packed in large common earthenware crocks. Fresh water is stored in wooden casks.

Especially important are the trade goods, beads, iron arrow points, tomahawk heads, blankets, and other goods which can be used to trade with the Indians. We will trade mostly for beaver furs. Other things we want from the Indians will also be traded for. The Indians don't use money, so we trade goods with them rather than buying from them. Even though the Indians don't use money to buy goods, sometimes they will take coins to use for decoration or jewelry.

Storage space is very limited on a ship, so every thing is stowed neatly and packed tightly. This also avoids having items damaged by being thrown about in bad weather.

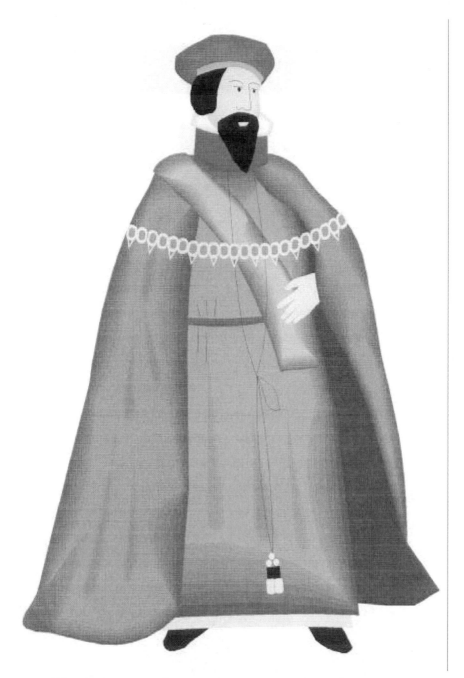

Sir John Popham watches carefully as provisions and weapons are loaded onto the ships.

Chapter 3

THE JOURNEY BEGINS

Today is the day we set sail, Tuesday, May 31, 1607.

I awaken very early this morning. My aunt has packed some special baked goods for me to take along and warns me to take care of myself and be careful. I grab my bundle of belongings and rush down to the dock.

When I arrive, the dock is quiet. Captain Popham is already on deck giving the ship a last going over. I quickly board.

Captain Popham says, "Welcome aboard, Benjamin! Stow your bundle in your quarters, and come back out on the main deck. Stay handy in case you're needed."

By high tide, the entire town of Plymouth is on the docks. Even Sir John Popham himself is there to see us off.

Sir John is busy with Captain Popham giving him last minute instructions. It's important that the construction of the new colony and fort goes smoothly.

Sir John addresses the crowd; "These fine brave men are embarking on a venture of great importance to the future of all English people. We wish the entire crew a safe and peaceful voyage, and Godspeed!"

Mr. Richard Seymour, our ship's chaplain conducts a short service asking God's blessings on the crew and ships.

Then Captain Popham gets the great ship under way. Orders are shouted, ropes are castoff, the seamen unfurl the huge sails and we are under way!

People on the docks are yelling and waving. Many people are crying. It may be a long time before loved ones are seen again. I can not believe we are actually on our way.

"Where are we heading?" I ask.

The Captain tells me, "We have set sail for the island of Flores. There we will make a stop to take on fresh water and firewood and then on to Virginia."

Captain Popham gets the great ships underway

Chapter 4

WHO IS THIS QUIET MAN?

I have met most of the crew, but there is one man I have not met. He is very quiet, rather tall and looks very strong. His skin is chestnut in color and he wears his long shiny black hair braided up in four parts, trussed around his head with a small knot behind. He seems to spend all his time looking out over the water. He doesn't smile or frown. He just looks.

I find him a bit scary and am glad he is traveling with Captain Gilbert instead of us.

Captain Popham tells me his name is Skidwares (Skidware'-iss). Skidwares is an Indian, from the Abenaki Tribe. He is one of five Indians captured by Captain Weymouth during his exploration voyage in 1605.

The Indians were taken from their home in America, back to England, where they lived for a time. Skidwares is educated in the English customs and speaks English.

He is to be our guide. His job is to help the colonists get along with the Indians who live in Virginia and help the colonists learn how to live in the New World.

Captain told me, "Be wary of him. He seems pleasant, but I am certain he resents being taken from his home. I don't feel he will be much help to us, but we shall see."

Skidwares is an Abinaki Indian. He was taken
to England and educated in the English
language and customs.

Chapter 5

LIFE ONBOARD THE GREAT SHIP

Soon we lose sight of the *Mary and John* and have no idea where they are or what has happened to them.

Life on the *Gift of God* is much different than at home.

The food is boring. We eat the same thing every day. Our menu consists of dried or salt cured meat and fish, biscuits, water, beer and wine. We have a cook stove on board, but many days the seas are too rough to use it.

Some days, if the sea is calm, we can catch and cook fish. This is a real treat. Most days dried or pickled food is the fare.

Bathing takes some getting used to. We have only enough fresh water for drinking, so we wash with sea-water.

At first I find washing in seawater leaves me feeling sticky. This objection quickly passes, and I come to look forward to a bath in seawater. One of the crew lowers a bucket on a rope over the side of the ship and dips water out of the sea. He then pours the water over the crew and passengers on the deck.

Bathing is done with clothes on, so clothes get washed at the same time. With the sun and sea breeze, it doesn't take long for us to dry off, including our clothes.

The privy is the same as at home, except the seat with the hole hangs over the bow or front of the ship, which I find very convenient.

Once the sails are set and we are on course, there is very little to do. The crew spends their free time carving, playing cribbage, and swapping sea yarns.

They tell each other stories of far away places they have visited, terrible storms at sea, huge monsters that swallow men in one gulp and voracious ship worms that eat the wood of the ship until the ship breaks apart and sinks.

I enjoy listening to the stories. Most of the yarns are interesting and fun. Some of the yarns are very scary and frighten me terribly! Some nights I dream about the ship breaking up and how horrible it would be!

Mr. Digby is a well-seasoned seaman and has become my friend. He always has time to talk with me. One afternoon I ask him, "Mr. Digby, are the stories the men tell true?" He knew I was upset.

Putting his large reassuring hand on my shoulder, he calmly said, "Benjamin, sometimes when men have too much time on their hands, their imaginations get away from them."

Sitting down on the deck, he continues, "Yes, we do have storms at sea. Some blow very long and very hard. But, with a good captain at the helm, we get through them. The important thing is to stay calm, batten the ship up tight, so we don't take on too much water and just ride the storm out."

"I've also seen some very large animals in the sea. They are whales. We will probably see some during our journey. As long as we leave them alone they don't bother us, and I have never ever seen them eat a sea-man," he said calmly, with a small smile on his face.

The Seamen tell stories of huge monsters
that swallow men in one gulp and
shipworms that eat ships.

He pulles me closer to him. "Now the sea worms," he says slowly, "Well, they are a different story. They are real. Being a ship's carpenter for a lot of years, I have repaired many ships with sea worm damage. The important thing is to check the ship and repair the sea worm damage before the beams get too weak."

"Sea worms make their homes inside of wood. They burrow through the beams and eat the wood. Their burrows weaken the wood. To keep them out of the wood, many ship hulls are coated with tar, pitch, copper or lead."

"Once sea worms are in the wood, a good captain can solve the problem. He will either sail the ship north into the cold water or up a large fresh water river and anchor the ship for a time. Sea worms cannot live in fresh or cold water."

Mr. Digby could tell by the look on my face that he had told me what I needed to hear. "Thank you sir. I was beginning to fear the sea, but now that I understand more about it, I feel much better."

Life on a ship at sea is a lot different than at home on land. There is no place to go, no privacy, space is very tight. I am the youngest crewmember and sometimes I miss having friends my own age. Often it is very boring with little to do.

But after I learn more about the ship and the sea and adjust to the routine, I begin to enjoy being at sea. My mind is always busy thinking about what life will be like in Virginia.

Chapter 6

THE MAIN LAND IS SIGHTED!

Early in the morning of July 30th, a cry comes from the crow's nest! "Land ho!"

Captain Popham advises the crew, "We have arrived at the main land and will soon be at our destination. All hands stay alert."

I ask Chaplain Seymour, "Why does the Captain sound so serious?"

Chaplain Seymour tells me, "Thank God we have arrived safely in Virginia. The longest part of our journey is behind us, but we are still faced with the perils of navigating the shores while we search for the mouth of the Sagadahoc River, where we are to build the colony."

"Why is navigating the shore so dangerous?" I ask. Chaplain Seymour explains, "There are many reasons, Benjamin. The ocean is shallow as we get near the land. The tide is very strong, sometimes rising or falling eight or nine feet through the day. The shoreline has many inlets and small islands. Shoals and large rocks can be hidden in the shallow waters. All hands must stay alert, because any of these dangers could seriously damage, or even sink, our fine ship if we should accidentally run up on one of them."

I appreciate the Chaplain's frank reply to my question, and now fully understand why there is always a reliable seaman in the crow's nest at all times while we are under way.

We have been worried about the ship *Mary and John*, and her crew. We haven't seen her in many weeks. We have arrived near our destination and are anchored off shore. Captain Popham and some of the crew have returned on board after exploring the shoreline.

Late one afternoon, the lookout in the crow's nest hollers, " Ahoy, there's a large vessel approaching. I can't see her flag."

Captain Popham shouts orders to the crew, "Prepare to defend the ship. It may be a Spanish ship and that would mean trouble!" As the ship approaches, the captain keeps close watch on her with his telescope. Captain Popham orders the crew, "She appears to be flying the English flag, but stay ready until we are certain!

Finally the captain yells, "I can see Captain Raleigh Gilbert waving from the bow of the ship. It is the *Mary and John*! They have crossed the sea safely and we are all together gain!" The crews of both ships are cheering and waving. What a happy time it is!

Captain Gilbert anchors near us. He and some of his crew lower a small boat and come on board our ship. We all spend several hours talking. The cook prepares a fine meal that night. Chaplain Seymour gives a lengthy blessing and gives thanks for our safekeeping and our success.

Captain Gilbert tells us, "Upon arriving, we were approached by a small band of Indians. At first we were wary. With the help of Skidwares, we peacefully traded knives and beads for beaver skins. I think Skidwares will be a big help!"

Captains Popham and Gilbert discuss the strategy they will use to locate our final destination. Because of the shallow waters, men set out in small boats to explore the inlets. They make careful charts and measure the water depth as they travel. We will need a deep channel to anchor the big ships.

Finally on August 19th the precise location for the Popham Colony is found. We all go onshore. Chaplain Seymour conducts a lengthy sermon, giving heart-felt thanks for the safe passage we have just completed. He asks that we are granted the strength, wisdom and guidance we will need in the weeks ahead. Building the fort and town is a formidable task.

The land patent from King James and the laws are read. Captain George Popham is elected President of the colony and Admiral Raleigh Gilbert is to be second in command.

Chapter 7

CONSTRUCTION BEGINS

Now that we have arrived in our new home and the formalities are completed, it is time to start work.

The following day, construction work begins. Most of the men are working at building the fort. We will be living on the ships until our buildings are built.

Mr. John Hunt, has been busy drawing the plan for the colony. I have been watching him, deep in thought, carefully considering each step of his design.

I asked Mr. Hunt, "Why don't we just build some homes and move into them?"

He patiently tells me, "Benjamin, many things have to be considered.

First, the Spanish are not pleased with our presence, and we are not certain about the Indians. A strong defense is the first consideration. The colony's location has been carefully chosen because it is easy to defend. It is located at the mouth of the Sagadahoc River. Being a large river, it is very important and anybody traveling up the river must pass us first.

At the south end of the fort is a high stone bluff upon which we will build President Popham's home. From this high point he will be able to keep an eye on the river.

We will also place our large cannons on the bluff. They can shoot all the way across the river, so we can fully defend the river."

"What about dangers coming from the land along the south and west sides of the fort?" I ask.

"Along these sides of the fort wc will build defensive walls called *ramparts*. *Ramparts* are built by digging a trench twenty feet wide and three feet deep. The dirt from the trench is piled up three feet high on the fort side of the trench. Thus, by digging a trench only three feet deep, we have built a wall, or *rampart*, six feet tall. An approaching enemy will face a wall six feet high from the bottom of the trench to the top of the dirt wall.

Our soldiers will be able to defend the fort from behind the ramparts. It will be similar to a moat around a castle. For added protection, we may place upright stakes with sharpened points on the top of the dirt wall."

Mr. Hunt continues, "The first building we must build is the storehouse. It will be a strong proper building because it will be very important. Here we will keep many of our important supplies. Our gunpowder and ammunition will be stored separately in the munitions house.

While one group of men is laying out the storehouse and digging holes where the main support posts will be placed, another group is busy cutting trees. The largest trees will be used as the main upright support posts. They will be set in the holes and back filled with earth to hold them in place. Smaller trees will be used for the walls and roof.

The next building we will build is the chapel. It too will be an important building and will be built with much care.

Finally the smaller storage buildings, homes and lesser buildings will be built."

Mr. Hunt says proudly, "When the colony is complete it will have fifty buildings surrounded with ramparts and defended with twelve cannons. What a fine fort we will have!"

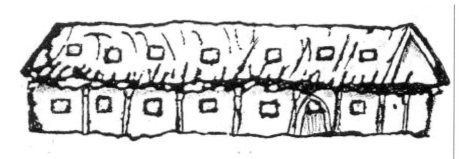

The First Building we must build is the Storehouse

The Chapel will be built with much care!

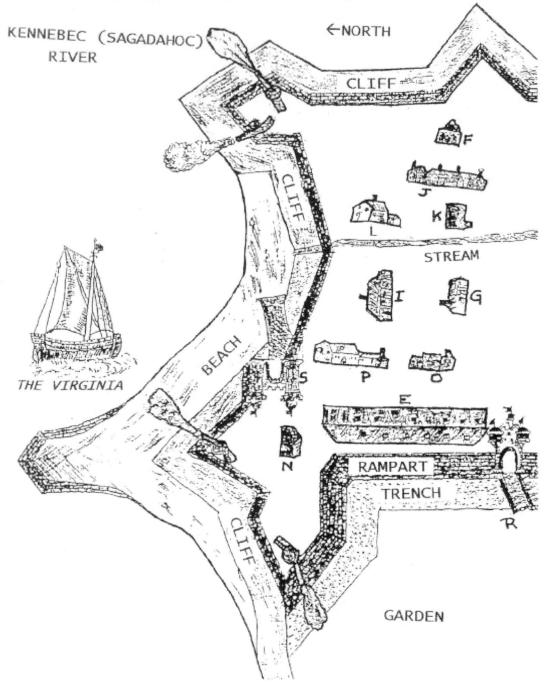

THE POPHAM COLONY

AS DRAWN BY MR. JOHN HUNT, 1607
MODIFIED BY AUTHOR FOR CLARITY

KENNEBEC (SAGADAHOC) RIVER

←NORTH

CLIFF

CLIFF

CLIFF

BEACH

STREAM

THE VIRGINIA

F

J

K

L

I

G

P

O

E

S

N

RAMPART

TRENCH

R

GARDEN

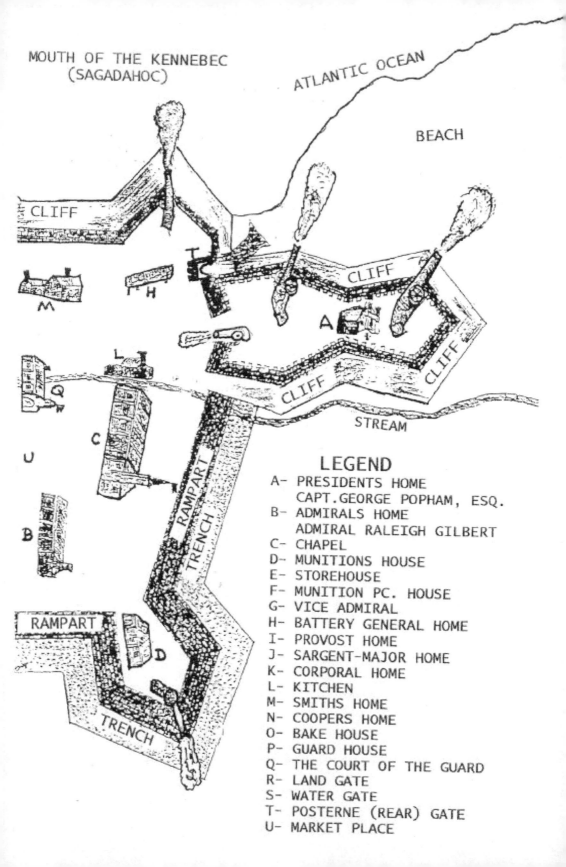

MOUTH OF THE KENNEBEC
(SAGADAHOC)

ATLANTIC OCEAN

BEACH

CLIFF

CLIFF

CLIFF

CLIFF

CLIFF

STREAM

RAMPART

TRENCH

RAMPART

TRENCH

LEGEND

A- PRESIDENTS HOME
   CAPT. GEORGE POPHAM, ESQ.
B- ADMIRALS HOME
   ADMIRAL RALEIGH GILBERT
C- CHAPEL
D- MUNITIONS HOUSE
E- STOREHOUSE
F- MUNITION PC. HOUSE
G- VICE ADMIRAL
H- BATTERY GENERAL HOME
I- PROVOST HOME
J- SARGENT-MAJOR HOME
K- CORPORAL HOME
L- KITCHEN
M- SMITHS HOME
N- COOPERS HOME
O- BAKE HOUSE
P- GUARD HOUSE
Q- THE COURT OF THE GUARD
R- LAND GATE
S- WATER GATE
T- POSTERNE (REAR) GATE
U- MARKET PLACE

Later, I ask President Popham, "What will my job be?" He tells me, "Benjamin, I need you down by the water helping Mr. Digby build our new ship. This is very important because, when our buildings are complete, *The Gift of God* and *Mary and John* will leave us and return to England. Our new ship will be our only means of travel. I know you and he are friends and you have a great fondness for ships. That is where you belong. Your job will be to help the men cut and shape the wooden timbers for the ship." President Popham is very careful in placing each man where he will do the most good for the colony.

Anxious to get to work, I immediately run down to the shore, Mr. Digby is explaining to his crew exactly how the new ship will be built and what each man's job will be. He sees me coming and says, "Welcome to my crew, Benjamin, your enthusiasm and strength is needed. Glad to have you!" He then continues telling us about the new ship. "When completed, she will be fifty feet in length and capable of carrying 30 tuns. A tun is a shipping container into which cargo is packed for shipping. She will be used to explore the coast, but will be capable of being rigged for sailing the open sea. She will be christened *The Virginia*, and she will be beautiful. Now, let's get her built!"

First Mr. Digby takes his crew into the forest and carefully selects each tree he will need for the new ship. He instructs us exactly how to cut and trim each tree. The work is hard and heavy, but I enjoy every bit of it. Being a part of such an important project is great fun.

Mr. Digby carefully selects each tree for *The Virginia* and instructs us exactly how to cut each timber.

"No need to carry useless wood all the way to the shore and waste time and energy. Work swiftly and carefully. I want the lumber taken from the forest to be properly cut to the size and shape we need," he commands.

Mr. Digby carefully selects the main bottom beam called a keel beam and lays it on the shore. The entire ship will be built on this beam. Then follows the ribs and framing of the hull. The large rudder is built and attached. The final work done on land is erecting the giant mast. It is dropped through an opening in the main deck and attached tightly to the keel beam.

To make the hull of the ship water tight, the joints between the rough hand cut planks need to be sealed. This sealing is called caulking. Caulking is done by pounding oakum tightly into the spaces between the planks. A tool called a caulking iron is used. Oakum is made from used hemp robe. The rope is untwisted and usually soaked in tree sap called pitch. If tar is available, it can also be used for making oakum. A caulking iron looks like a wood chisel with a broad flat blade and is flat on the working end rather than sharp.

The first part of the ship we build is the hull. Building the hull will take about four weeks. When the hull is completed, and is able to float, it will be launched into the bay and tied up to the dock. The decking, and rigging will be completed while the hull is floating in the water tied to the dock. If we built the entire ship on land it would very heavy and difficult to launch.

The Virginia of Sagadahoc

Chapter 8

WE GIVE THANKS

We have been at work almost three months. The storehouse is well built and weather tight. Several homes have been built. The walls and ramparts of the fort are done and our cannons are in place. We can now unload the ships and carefully store our valuable provisions safely away.

Our new colony is almost complete. It will soon be time for the tall ships to return to England.

President Popham declares a thanksgiving feast day to celebrate our successes. He sends a message to Skidwares and the Indians to join in our feast. Even with their reluctance, they have been very helpful. Their trading with us has provided profitable trade goods to send back to England, as well as sorely needed food. They have also helped us learn about our new home. We want them to be our friends and neighbors.

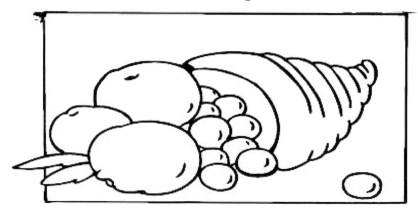

Skidwares and many Abenaki's arrive early on the thanksgiving feast day, bearing cooked venison, smoked oysters and squash.

In the new chapel, Chaplain Seymour conducts an inspiring service. Our Indian friends are invited. Even though few of them understand English, they silently attend our religious service with respect and silence.

The feast is a grand time. We enjoy the venison, oysters and squash from our Indian guests, as well as corn bread, fish, fowl, cooked cranberries sweetened with honey, and finish up with grape and blueberry pies.

The language barrier soon disappears into smiles and gestures of good will. After the meal, the Indians present us a special gift of cured tobacco.

In return, Captain Popham gives our guests English clay pipes. We all smoke this special gift. The Indians use pipes made of stone with hollow wood stems. We use our clay pipes. Surprisingly, some of the Indians use pipes made of hollow lobster claws. I have not smoked a pipe before and the experience is very interesting, especially sharing it with Skidwares and his Abenaki friends!

It is dark when the festivity ends, and we bid our Indian friends farewell.

The feast is a complete success. Besides the enjoyment, several of the men who had been very suspicious of the Indians seem to now have better feelings about them. We will all sleep well tonight!

Chapter 9

ALONE IN OUR NEW HOME

With our new colony almost complete and our supplies unloaded, it is time for the tall ships and their crews to leave us and return to England.

Mr. Hunt's work is done. His plan is completed and he will be going back to England.

I approach Mr. Hunt, "Sir, I wish you a safe journey home. You have taught me much about the fort and I appreciate the time you have spent with me."

"Benjamin, use what you have learned. The Popham Colony is only the beginning. Soon many more colonists will arrive. Virginia is a large area and will someday be a large and valuable addition to the British Empire. Your knowledge may come in very handy."

With that, Mr. Hunt extends his hand to mine and we shake. I am smiling on my face, but I am sad inside. Somehow I know this is the last time we will see each other.

Most of the men will return to England leaving forty-five men at The Popham Colony.

President Popham has prepared a letter to King James telling him of our accomplishments and great expectations. We have found grapes, both red and white, hops, onions, garlic, oak, cedar and walnut trees, furs, skins, sassafras, and good soil for crops.

The Indians tell us there is a large body of water to the west only a few days travel up river. Our maps indicate this is most likely the waterway to the Far East. The Far East is an important source of spices and silk. Profitable trade with the Far East has been conducted for many years. The known routes, both across land and by sea are very long and extremely dangerous.

If this new route is a shorter way to the Far East, it will be to our great advantage. We could profit greatly from this trade. We will explore this as soon as time and weather allow.

As the ships leave us, I feel all alone. But my loneliness quickly leaves me as I turn around and marvel at the fine fort we have built in the last three months, complete with our fine ship *The Virginia* floating at the dock. We are ready to start our new lives!

Chapter 10

THE TERRIBLE WINTER

Sitting on the rampart looking out to sea, I am worried. The ocean is changing. Its beautiful friendly blue color is gone. Now it is a mean dark gray-green. The large white waves are crashing and attacking the shore as if they are very angry.

President Popham approaches me looking concerned, and says, "Winter is coming sooner than I planned. It is only November and we have heavy snow on the ground. I wouldn't have expected this weather until late December. The east winds are blowing very hard and the gray sky looks as if more snow is on the way."

"Yes Sir," I agree, "The weather is getting very cold and the wind blows constantly."

"Sir", I ask, "The charts show we are located in the same latitude north as Spain. Why is it so much colder here than in Spain?" Captain Popham pauses a while before answering my question. He replies, "Benjamin, there are many things we do not know. Your reasoning is sound. Generally the farther south we travel, the warmer the weather becomes. As you can see, there are no palm trees here as there are in Spain, nor are the soil or geography the same. We shall see what the winter holds for us."

I didn't sleep well that night. I thought Captain

Popham knew everything. If he doesn't have answers who does?

The following morning, I see Master Gome Carew on the deck of *The Virginia* examining his maps. His job is the "Chief Searcher". Maybe he can answer some questions for me. "Master Carew" I inquire, " Would you be so kind as to answer a question for me. There is something worrying me." "Certainly Benjamin," he replies, "Come sit here and tell me what troubles you." I relate yesterday's conversation with Captain Popham.

Master Carew is a calm man. He is a man who seems to be able to handle anything. His presence on the ship is reassuring for me. "Benjamin," he says, " there are many things we do not know about this new land. My job, no, our job, is very important for the future of Virginia. We must find answers to as many of these questions as we are able. Our job is to gather information so the colonists who come to Virginia after us will know better what to expect. We are colonists, but we are also explorers. This is an important mission we are on!"

Master Carew continues, "Benjamin, we don't know what we face. We have the finest group of men Sir John could assemble for this noble adventure. We must be brave, careful and pay very close attention to what is happening around us. If we do these things, we will be as safe as brave men can be doing a dangerous job."

"Wow!" I think, "I never thought of myself as an explorer!" The unknown is not to be feared it is a challenge to be carefully and thoroughly investigated.

Future colonists will rely on what we learn from our experience. They will plan their ventures based on what we discover. Our exploration will make the New World safer for those who follow us!

As winter sets in, the snow comes faster and heavier than I have ever seen. Our Indian neighbors disappear into the interior of the forest. Skidwares has gone with them.

I never really got to know Skidwares. He didn't seem to be friendly, but he was never unfriendly either. We

**Winter is coming sooner than expected.
It is only November and we have heavy
snow on the Ground!**

saw him several times after he left. When the Indians would come to trade, he would come with them. He would translate and take care of business, but never had anything else to say.

He always went home with the Indians. When I saw him sometimes our eyes would meet. I would smile, but he would just look at me. I feel he did not like and did not trust President Popham and the rest of the men. I suspect Mr. John Hunt was right when he told me, Skidwares knew, "Soon many more colonists will arrive!"

Even with our shelters built, it is impossible to keep warm. Life is very hard.

The deep snow makes walking difficult. Working is almost impossible.

Supplies we felt ample soon prove to be woefully inadequate. Food and firewood supplies are dangerously low.

Making matters more difficult, Admiral Gilbert's home catches on fire and is almost totally destroyed. We are able to rebuild the home in a few days, but the lost supplies cannot be replaced.

In February of 1608 President George Popham is taken seriously ill and dies. He will be missed greatly. The entire crew admired and depended on him. He was a well-experienced leader, treated the men fairly, and was very slow to anger. His calm manner kept the construction of the colony progressing smoothly. He quickly settled any arguing or bickering that might occur.

With the ground frozen solid, we decide to bury him in the dirt floor of the chapel. Chaplain Seymour conducts the service.

The loss of President Popham leaves Admiral Gilbert in charge of the colony. Admiral Gilbert is a totally different kind of man. He is strong headed, very ambitious and demanding. He does not seem to care if the men like him or not. While these traits may sound undesirable, he faces a very difficult task. His strength will serve him well. He and President Popham disagreed on many things, but I think the Admiral misses the President's wise council in these most difficult times.

The following weeks are horrible. The cold bitter winter continues to bury us in snow. The wind blows constantly and causes the snow to pile in high drifts making work or even walking almost impossible.

We cannot get out to the forest to collect firewood. Often we run out of firewood and spend the night without a fire. Food is frighteningly low and tightly rationed. Work on the fort is completely stopped.

When a break in the weather allows us to get outside, all our time is needed to collect firewood and look for food.

Besides being hungry and cold, the men are very discouraged. We are kept inside for days at a time with little or nothing to do. Many of the men are weak and sick. The winter seems to last forever.

Finally winter starts to ease up a little. The snow and wind decrease. We are all encouraged with the first signs of spring. The trees are turning green. Animals start returning to the shore. Spirits improve and we are able to get out to hunt and gather food.

On a sunny afternoon in mid April we receive an unexpected visit from Skidwares. He seems surprised to find us alive. We tell him of George Pophams death and the terrible time we experienced.

Skidwares asks us why we stayed on the shore through the winter. He explains that he and the entire Abenaki people go inland for the winter to seek protection from the cold weather. Away from the shore the wind is not so severe and the game is slightly more plentiful.

Skidwares continues to explain to us that he and his people also struggle through the winters. They refer to late winter as "the starving time". After several weeks of snow and cold they also run low on food. They often make soup by boiling leather in water and may live on this for a month or more while waiting for the spring to arrive.

With the good weather they return to the shore with it's ample supply of seafood and plant their gardens. Skidwares tells us the summer is good to the Abenakis.

The summer is good for us also. We are able to find game and like Skidwares and the Abenaki people, we too plant our garden. Soon we have all the food we need and life is good.

Work on the fort continues and we have a very pleasant summer.

Chapter 11

RETURN TO ENGLAND

Early in September 1608, our supply ship arrives from England. The captain has much news.

First, Sir John Popham has died in a riding accident at his home in Wellington. Sir John was our colony's main promoter and financial backer. His death is terrible news. His heir is his son Sir Francis Popham. Sir Francis has taken charge of the Popham interests but he has no way to know of President Popham's death.

Second, Admiral Gilbert's brother has died as well, leaving The Admiral heir to a large estate in England. The Admiral has to choose between returning to England to live the life of a gentleman or facing another bitter winter at The Popham Colony. His decision is swift. He immediately prepares to return to England.

With no leadership the colony is in peril. There is much confusion and concern among the colonists. Many of them have no reason to return to England. Some talk of staying. To them, Virginia is their only opportunity to become wealthy.

There is much talk about whether to continue the colony. Without President George Popham's leadership and encouragement and with the financial backing of Sir John Popham being uncertain, many of the colonists are afraid to stay. Sir John has been a main financial backer of the colony and his death leaves many questions as to how much future support the Popham Colony will receive from England. The colony is not yet strong enough to survive without supplies from England. Benjamin has mixed feelings about returning to England. He has grown fond of his new home and thought he would live in the Popham Colony permanently. The thought of abandoning his new home and all their hard work makes him sad. But, it has been over a year since he has seen his family and friends in the West Country of England and he would love to see them again. The colonists reluctantly decide to abandon the colony and return to England. Their remaining supplies are loaded aboard the supply ship and aboard *The Virginia*. Benjamin and the other colonists board the ships and regretfully leave the Popham Colony. Captain Davies will have the privilege of captaining *The Virginia* on her first voyage across the Atlantic.

Chapter 12

WHAT DO I DO NOW?

Back in England, my future is uncertain. I am sitting on the dock watching the fabulous tall ships and thinking about what I will do.

The captain of *The Virginia* sees me and calls me over. He and his crew are taking a large cargo of provisions back to Jamestown.

The captain asks, "Benjamin, would you care to sail to Jamestown with me? Your familiarity with *The Virginia* and your experience of twice crossing the Atlantic will be very valuable to me. Besides, if you are man enough to be chosen by Captain Popham, I am certain you will make an excellent seaman." My decision doesn't take long. "Yes Sir, I will be very pleased to sail to Jamestown with you and your crew."

The word "seaman" keeps going through my head. On this voyage, I will be sailing as a real seaman.

Our trip to Jamestown begins at high tide on a bright sunny day. *The Virginia* is handling unusually well with a strong even wind blowing behind her and a well-seasoned crew on board. "What a fine trip this will be!" I think. I was very wrong!

During the third week of our voyage the weather conditions start to change. The pleasant even wind turns blustery with gusts so strong The Captain orders our sails lowered and all cargo checked to make sure it is well secured. The sky is heavy with dark fast moving clouds!

The water is now dark gray with the biggest white-capped waves I have ever seen! The crew is very concerned and the rough water has many sick. The cook can not prepare meals, but none of the crew is hungry.

The Captain warns, "We are in for some rough weather! *The Virginia* is a fine seaworthy ship and we will be safe as long as we all stay calm and follow orders."

Weather conditions deteriorate quickly! Soon heavy rain is falling. *The Virginia* is very seaworthy, but The Captain has men stationed below deck in the hold ready to bail out any water we may take on. It is not long before they are bailing.

The wind and rain are blowing so hard it is impossible to see on deck and all that can are huddled below deck in the hold. I feel helpless as we are thrown about. The huge waves are crashing high over the bow of the ship. Every person on board is hanging on and praying. We are in a full-blown hurricane!

The storm rages on for three horrid days and three terrifying nights.

On the fourth day, the weather finally starts to calm down. Rain is still falling, but the men no longer need to bail water out of the hold. The wind is still too blustery to raise the sails, but we can now get up on the deck.

As I climb up out of the hold, I do not believe my eyes. Our beloved *Virginia* has suffered severe damage from the hurricane. Our rigging is a mess and some of the spars have been damaged. Luckily the masts are in serviceable condition.

Even though *The Virginia* has suffered damage from our ordeal, she did her job well. The crew is safe, no lives are lost and no one is seriously injured.

As I survey *The Virginia's,* storm damage I appreciate the many days I spent with Mr. Digby building this fine ship. I know her well from stem to stern and know how each piece was made and installed.

I am neither the oldest nor the most experienced man on the crew, but I know what has to be done.

The Captain calls me to his quarters. He orders, "Benjamin, you are in charge of getting *The Virginia* back into shape. Take charge of the crew and make quick work of the needed repairs! We have several days to make up for and I have to figure out where we are so I can get us back on course."

Back on deck I get the crew started on the needed repairs. Several men are sent up into the rigging to get it untangled. Others are sent below for tools and supplies.

After I get the topside repairs under way, I turn my attention to the most important item, the rudder. Without the rudder the ship cannot be sailed.

I inspect the rudder very thoroughly. It is in fine condition and operates perfectly. With heart felt appreciation I whisper, "Thank goodness!" Damaged rudders are difficult or sometimes impossible to repair at sea.

Soon needed repairs are complete and *The Virginia* is ready to continue our voyage. The Captain has our course laid out and we are underway.

Our arrival at Jamestown has been greatly delayed. We arrive just in time to meet the Jamestown colonists sailing down the James River to the sea. Conditions at Jamestown are terrible. Provisions have run out and many men have died.

They too have decided to give up their venture and return to England. With the new provisions however, the colonists are ordered to turn around and stay on.

Jamestown has ample fresh provisions and is safe for now, but as we learned at the Popham Colony, life in the New World is harsh, unforgiving and has constant unexpected surprises.

As we prepare for the return trip to England I feel fully capable of handling the job of a seaman.

Where will my future take me? I wonder. Maybe I will go up to North Virginia. Since the death of Sir John, his son Sir Francis Popham has carried on a profitable trade in the area called Pemaquid. Yes, I like that idea. I will contact Sir Francis as soon as I get back to England. I'm certain he can use an experienced able-bodied seaman like myself.

The sea is now my home and I cannot wait to see where my next journey takes me.

The sea is now my home, and I cannot wait to
see where my next journey takes me.

Postscript

by Dr. Jeffrey P. Brain, Archaeologist

If Benjamin lived among us today, he might very well become an archaeologist. Just as he set forth four centuries ago to seek adventure, so the modern archaeologist sets forth to explore the people, places and events of centuries past. Archaeological adventure has all the excitement of learning something new (even when it is old!), and if the explorer is lucky he or she makes discoveries more rewarding than golden treasures.

The archeological discovery of the Popham Colony, where Benjamin discovered a new world, has been one of these exciting adventures. Although Popham was the first English colony in New England, being founded in 1607, thirteen years before the Pilgrims came to these shores, it had been all but forgotten because it failed after a year and the colonists sailed back home in 1608. Even the very site of their settlement, which they called Fort St. George, had been lost to memory. As Benjamin describes, here was an event that participated with Jamestown in the foundation of English America, yet we did not even know where the colonists had settled. If we could find this site, so important to the history of our country, then we could excavate it and learn how these earliest colonists lived.

The map of Fort St. George drawn by John Hunt provided the first clues. The unusual shape of the fort suggested that it had been built to conform to a particular piece of land, and we searched until we found a spot that seemed to fit. But there was no indication of a fort to be seen, so then we began excavating to see if we could find remains of it preserved underground. We dug for weeks before we were rewarded with evidence left by the Popham colonists. They had indeed built a fort there. It was hard to see because the walls had been made of earth, not stone masonry, and the houses and other buildings were made of wood that had quickly rotted away.

The colonists had arrived late in the summer and they had to rush to complete their simple fort and housing before the harsh New England winter arrived. We learned that they had been short of food and had to hunt and fish and trade with the Indians to get enough to eat. The colonists were all men or boys for there were no women in this first settlement. Most of the men were soldiers and we found many pieces of armor, guns and lead bullets. But there were also carpenters, who built the houses, and shipwrights, who built the little boat *Virginia*. We even found a shipbuilding tool. We found that some men were more important than others. The leaders lived in bigger houses, had more food, dressed better, and were supplied with the best arms and other equipment. We also discovered that much of the fort had burned, at least some of it while the colonists were still living there. We don't know whether it was an accidental burning, or perhaps the result of an Indian raid, but it surely contributed to the eventual failure of the colony.

All together, we are walking where those colonists walked, we are touching the very objects they last handled 400 years ago, and we are sharing some of their experience. In short, we are learning what it was like. The adventure continues.

Postscript

by Mr. Bud Warren
of *Maine's First Ship*

Benjamin watched Master Digby and the shipwrights build the pinnace *Virgnia.*

Completing *Virginia* was an important event, for it was:
- England's first major industrial activity in the New World
- The first English ship built on the North American continent.
- The beginning of New England's long record of shipbuilding.
- Maine's first ship.

Virginia was probably the Popham Colony's greatest success.

The few documents that remain suggest that right from the start, the founders of the colony planned to build a vessel. They put Digby, a London shipwright, in charge of construction. He and his workers started work very shortly after they arrived in August of 1607.

Virginia was a "pinnace" – a small, square-ended sailing vessel, capable of being rowed or sailed. Described as being some 30 tons, the crage would have been about 50 feet in length. She would have been a typical workboat of the early 17th century. She would have met the many different needs of the new settlement: exploring the coast, exploration, carrying cargoes, perhaps even fishing.

When the colony was abandoned in 1608, some of the settlers sailed *Virginia* to England. The following year she re-crossed the Atlantic, carrying 16 passengers and crew to Jamestown, Fort St. George's sister colony further south.

Records show that *Virginia* served the Jamestown colony in 1609 and 1610. She was even being made ready to cross the Atlantic Ocean a third time when the Jamestown colonists were preparing to abandon their settlement.

Nothing more is known about this little craft.

For years, people in Maine have had a warm place in their hearts for this ship, the first ever built on their shores. In 1997 a group met at the site of Fort St. George and decided to build a new *Virginia* to honor her and those who built her. They formed an organization now known as Maine's First Ship to create a reconstruction of *Virginia*.

The design of the new *Virginia* is based on seven years of study. Because so few records exist, no one knows what the original ship looked like. Much time has been spent in England and here in America searching to find out. Paintings, drawings, letters and printed material about early 17th century vessels have been thoroughly researched. Two naval architects have worked to design the new *Virginia*. It will not be a replica, for there is nothing to "replicate," to copy. It will be a "reconstruction." That means it will be as close as possible to the kind of pinnace a shipwright from London would have built in 1607. Benjamin would feel right at home on her.

The new *Virginia* will be built and launched by 2007, in time to celebrate the 400th anniversary of the colony of which Benjamin was a part. *Virginia* will sail proudly along the coast of Maine just as the original did in 1607 and 1608. She will be a symbol of America's great shipbuilding tradition. Young people of Benjamin's age will be able to sail on her and learn first-hand what he knew so well.

Maine's First Ship's website is www.mainesfirst-ship.org.